Sammy the Silly Sausage

PHASE 5

6b

Level 6 – Orange

one and

BookLife

Helpful Hints for Reading at Home

The graphemes (written letters) and phonemes (units of sound) used throughout this series are aligned with Letters and Sounds. This offers a consistent approach to learning whether reading at home or in the classroom. Books levelled as 'a' are an introduction to this band. Readers can advance to 'b' where graphemes are consolidated and further graphemes are introduced.

HERE IS A LIST OF NEW GRAPHEMES FOR THIS PHASE OF LEARNING. AN EXAMPLE OF THE PRONUNCIATION CAN BE FOUND IN BRACKETS.

Phase 5			
ay (day)	ou (out)	ie (tie)	ea (eat)
oy (boy)	ir (girl)	ue (blue)	aw (saw)
wh (when)	ph (photo)	ew (new	oe (toe)
au (Paul)	a_e (make)	e_e (these)	i_e (like)
o_e (home)	u_e(rule)		

HERE ARE SOME WORDS WHICH YOUR CHILD MAY FIND TRICKY.

Phase 5 Tricky Words			
oh	their	people	Mr
Mrs	looked	called	asked
could			

HERE ARE SOME WORDS THAT MIGHT NOT YET BE FULLY DECODABLE.

Challenge Words			
Sammy	silly	sausage	clumsy

TOP TIPS FOR HELPING YOUR CHILD TO READ:

• Allow children time to break down unfamiliar words into units of sound and then encourage children to string these sounds. together to create the word.

• Encourage your child to point out any focus phonics when they are used.

• Read through the book more than once to grow confidence.

• Ask simple questions about the text to assess understanding.

• Encourage children to use illustrations as prompts.

This book is a 'b' level and is an orange level 6 book band.

Sammy the Silly Sausage

Written by
Shalini Vallepur

Illustrated by
Simona Hodonova

Sammy dropped things and tripped over her feet all the time. Look out, Sammy!

Sammy was clumsy. She got called a silly sausage by her friends, her teacher and her mum all the time. But Sammy just smiled.

"Sammy, you are a silly sausage!" Mum said to Sammy one morning.
"I was trying to make you some toast, Mum," Sammy said.

The toast Sammy had made for Mum was black and burnt. Sammy had tried to make something that tasted good for her mum. Things never went right.

One day, Sammy and her friends were playing at the park. Sammy went up a tree. She went high up, right to the treetop.
"Sammy, what are you doing?" called Sammy's friend. "You might fall!"

There was a gust of wind and Sammy fell off the treetop. She landed right on her bum.

On another day, Sammy and her friends were playing on the street. It started to rain but Sammy did not have her raincoat.

"Run! Run!" her friends yelled.
"Wait for me!" Sammy said. Sammy started
to run after her friends, but she tripped. She
started to weep and her leg started to bleed.

Sammy went home. Her feet were wet, and she was sad. "What is the matter, sausage?" Mum asked.

"I am sick of being a silly sausage, Mum.
I keep getting hurt," said Sammy.
"It's okay, Sammy," said Mum with a sigh.

That night, Mum tucked Sammy into bed. Mum hugged Sammy and pulled the sheets up to her chin. "Sleep tight, Sammy," Mum said.

"I keep getting hurt and things never go right. I am sick of being a silly sausage," said Sammy.

Sammy was tucked up tight in bed. She began to drift off into a deep sleep.

When she woke up, Sammy tried to get out of bed, but she started to roll.

Sammy looked down and saw that she had turned into a sausage! And she was not in her bed – she was in a cooking pan! She was having a bad dream.

In a flash, Sammy was on the treetop at the park. "Why am I in the tree?" she said.

There was a bird in the nest that was looking for food. It saw Sammy and came closer. "How rude! Ow!" Sammy fell off the branch.

Sammy was on the street again. She saw her friends running away from the rain. She went to run and jump after them, but she fell over and started to roll. Sammy rolled and rolled and rolled down the street.

Sammy did not stop rolling down the street.
And in fact, Sammy hoped she did not stop!

"Weee! This is fun, I want to keep rolling!" said Sammy. She was spinning, rolling, twirling and flipping all the way down the road.

Sammy woke up at home with a smile on her face. She looked down to see that she was a person again. She was amazed.

"It was okay being a sausage. I had a lot of fun," said Sammy.

The next morning, Mum came down to a shock. There was toast with lots of jam, and a mug of coffee waiting for her.

"Sammy, did you make this for me?" asked
Mum.
"Yes, I did. I tried my best to make it for you,
Mum! It is okay being a sausage, just not
a silly one!" said Sammy.

"Thank you, sausage!" said Mum. She gave Sammy a big hug.

Sammy the Silly Sausage

1. What did Sammy do to the toast she made for Mum?

2. How do you think Sammy felt about being clumsy?

3. What does Sammy turn into in her bad dream?

   (a) A noodle

   (b) A sausage

   (c) A banana

4. What did Sammy make for Mum the next morning?

5. What do you think Sammy learned from her bad dream? How do you think you would feel if you were Sammy?

©2020 **BookLife Publishing Ltd.**
King's Lynn, Norfolk PE30 4LS

ISBN 978-1-83927-300-1

Sammy the Silly Sausage
Written by Shalini Vallepur
Illustrated by Simona Hodonova

An Introduction to BookLife Readers...

Our Readers have been specifically created in line with the London Institute of Education's approach to book banding and are phonetically decodable and ordered to support each phase of the Letters and Sounds document.

Each book has been created to provide the best possible reading and learning experience. Our aim is to share our love of books with children, providing both emerging readers and prolific page-turners with beautiful books that are guaranteed to provoke interest and learning, regardless of ability.

BOOK BAND GRADED using the Institute of Education's approach to levelling.

PHONETICALLY DECODABLE supporting each phase of Letters and Sounds.

EXERCISES AND QUESTIONS to offer reinforcement and to ascertain comprehension.

BEAUTIFULLY ILLUSTRATED to inspire and provoke engagement, providing a variety of styles for the reader to enjoy whilst reading through the series.

AUTHOR INSIGHT:
SHALINI VALLEPUR

Passionate about books from a very young age, Shalini Vallepur received the award of Norfolk County Scholar for her outstanding grades. Later on she read English at the University of Leicester, where she stayed to complete her Modern Literature MA. Whilst at university, Shalini volunteered as a Storyteller to help children learn to read, which gave her experience and expertise in the way children pick up and retain information. She used her knowledge and her background and implemented them in the 32 books that she has written for BookLife Publishing. Shalini's writing easily takes us to different worlds, and the serenity and quality of her words are sure to captivate any child who picks up her books.

PHASE 5

6b

This book is a 'b' level and is an orange level 6 book band.